CW00632105

Peeling Back the Years // Lemon Tree Writers

Peeling Back the Years

Celebrating 30 Years of Prose & Poetry by
Lemon Tree Writers

Published by Lemon Tree Writers in 2023
lemontreewriters.wordpress.com

Copyright remains with the respective authors

Book design by Lumphanan Press
www.lumphananpress.co.uk

ISBN: 978-0-9930319-4-6

Printed by Imprint Digital, UK

The Selectors: Bernard Briggs, Richie Brown, Aidan Mulkerrin (prose),
Cat Brown, Eddie Gibbons, Knotbrook Taylor (poetry).
The Editors: Brenda Conn & Martin Walsh.
Editorial assistants: Sandra Davison, Rik Gammack, Zusana Storrier

Lemon Tree Writers thank all members of the editorial team for their time
and dedication in helping to bring *Peeling Back the Years* to publication.

Contents

With the Gaiety, If You Know What I Mean

Foreword by Todd McEwen

In my first few days in Aberdeen, I was one evening in the The Grill, a resort of journalists and other undesirables. I was talking with one of them, an affable, shabby chap from the Press & Journal. He got around to asking me what I did and when I told him I was the new Writer in Residence, he twitched, gave me the blankest look I've ever seen, and abandoned the bar and his drink without saying a word.

The night I had arrived, I was in a hotel in Crown Street. The weather was wet. Big surprise. At about two o'clock in the morning, there was a disturbance outside. I looked down into the street and there was a guy with a shaven head following another guy, saying 'Yeu block bostord. Yeu block bostord', over and over again. He said it about six thousand times.

I was invited to write something for The Leopard, a local magazine. I submitted a piece about Crown Street and the block bostord. The editor told me she 'couldn't understand' it.

On the Fourth of July I had a picnic in Duthie Park with two American friends. The hailstones were the size of golf balls, and they haven't spoken to me since.

But, for the most part, these turned out to be the only adverse experiences I had in Aberdeen, unless you count the overly numerous and uncomfortable chairs in the Board Room of the Central Library. Even though it was a grand room, there were too many chairs and it was quite amusing each week to watch us all try to sit down.

The ancient formality of the Board Room was a striking contrast to the writers who came to the group we began there, a fantastically lively, varied bunch – this was an unexpected side to Aberdeen: despite its capitalist weirdness and royalist history, the place can be diverse.

All these interested and talented writers – from all over Scotland of course, but also from Sudan, France, South Africa, Texas, Orkney, Liverpool... Not only did they read what I asked them to, which hardly ever bloody happens, but they really wrote, sincerely and freely. Wonderfully. Nothing could have pleased me more. And they became my friends.

Residencies are demanding. On the last day of my post I was having lunch with one of the writers, and I could barely lift my sandwich. I began to lean toward the left. 'Are you all right?' he asked. I said, 'Oh, I'm just happy.'

– *Todd McEwen, Aberdeen Writer in Residence 1993-94,*
  whose workshops presaged Lemon Tree Writers.

The End of Poetry // *Eddie Gibbons*

One of the secret powers of this poem
is to render the reader's clothing invisible.

This may account for the occasional
cries of alarm heard in Public Libraries.

So be careful where you read these words.
And next time you see someone bare

and oblivious in a bookshop stay calm.
Close the book and lead them gently

from the Poetry shelves, avoiding
the Children's section, and usher them

to the Meet-the-Author stand
where they will form a nude tableau entitled:

Reading Poetry Is Like Standing Naked In Front
Of People And Baring Your Soul To Them.

Let them become aware of each other's bodies.
Let them begin where all poems end.

A Mention of My Father

Leila Aboulela

When my father died, I found it preposterous that we should leave him in a graveyard, that we should cover him with sand and just walk away. He, who used to shower and change twice a day, pat his chin with expensive eau de cologne, wear nothing that was not freshly ironed. Sparkling white shirts without a speck of dust, the fashionable suits he travelled in, shining shoes. It seemed to me outrageous that he would be left to fend for himself in the outskirts of Omdurman, without his radio, his Guardian overseas edition, his tiny notebook in which he wrote in careful, beautiful script the telephone numbers of everyone he valued.

My father was buried in the family graveyard, right next to his brother, close to his cousins and other brothers. It was where he would have wanted to be. A place that was completely his, of him, close to where he was born and grew up. A place he had visited time and again. It had good vibes, generations of the same family, thick bloodlines and continuity. I liked its peaceful, expansive atmosphere, its laden histories, but still when the day came to leave my father there, where he now belonged, it felt like a violation. The freshly dug sand moist and dark above his grave rose puckered like a troubled wound.

A couple of years earlier, my father and I had gone together to the graveyard, so that I could pay my respects to all the uncles and aunts who had died while I was away. My father sat on the ledge of his brother's grave, in the same spot where he was later buried. He was matter of fact, not unduly sentimental. Although it was a sombre visit, there was still between us the happiness that I, my husband and children were visiting from abroad. In our honour, my father had put up new curtains in the house, made sure all the light bulbs were working, spread new sheets on the beds. Throughout my childhood only important guests got this treatment. To my delight, I had become one of them.

My father died in 2008. If he were to come back to life now, there would be lots to explain. He had missed out on Obama as president, WhatsApp, China in Africa, Islamophobia (the word not the concept), Brexit (the word not the concept), #MeToo (not the concept of course); he had missed out on Dubai as a holiday destination, the secession of South Sudan, a Muslim mayor for London, the weak sterling, the hotter summers, Egyptians keeping pets, Netflix, online shopping, the Arab spring, the Asian Tiger, the Syrian civil war, the Indonesian tsunami and the overthrow of Omar el Bashir. He had missed out on the virus. Corona, I would say, yes, remember Mama's car, it's spreading, there's a lockdown. And no, even the West does not have a cure, believe it or not, even Europeans are dying in the thousands though with stiff upper lips and there is public anger but no signs of grief. 'I don't believe you, Leila,' he would say. 'You're talking nonsense.'

To reassure him, because I wouldn't want him to be frightened, I wouldn't want to spoil the mood, the special event of his coming back to life, I would say the tennis at Wimbledon is still going strong, the power cuts, Ethiopian Airlines; The Guardian is still going strong. I had never forgotten his special weekly overseas edition, its pages' tissues folded small in an envelope. His lovely trust in it; the pleasure he took in the rustle of its fragility. 'Look,' I would say, 'how much I am like you now!' Reaching out for my phone first thing in the morning, scrolling for the news. He used to balance his transistor radio on his stomach. It was the first sound I heard waking up, the reassuring pompous notes of the BBC World Service.

If my father were to come back to life, there would be a lot to say. How my children were doing, what they were up to, now that they were young adults. I would brag about how much like him I had become. Who could have seen that coming? I too feel shy in the company of my children's spouses, I too travel with ease, am wary of escalators, love a good gossip. I too am baffled by aggression; I too can't be bothered with small details or going out of my way to eat special things. I too get moody on my own unless I am reading. My hair hasn't yet turned white and my neck and shoulders ache. I too am perplexed by zippers and changing batteries, for him it was the batteries of torches and remote controls, for me it is the batteries of card readers and fashion watches. But I imagine my father, now back to life, would become restless and unsettled. Where are my brothers, he would ask? Where is my best friend, my crowd, the movers and shakers, the ones with the news, where are my people?

He grew up in a teaming household, ten brothers and sisters, countless cousins, innumerable friends. The nuclear family remained a novelty to him. On my own, I was never enough to hold his attention, not obtrusive enough. I was small in his eyes and only big in his heart, valuable but a responsibility. Finding himself in the 2020s, he would want to return to a world in which he was young again. Not be a father to a middle-aged woman.

And true I was like him. I too would want to return to the past, my past, to be with him when he knew everything, and I knew little. Before I had the choice and ability to disobey him. Before I started to needle him, to talk back, like girls talk back, sly, sharp, judgemental. I wasted so much time, not arguing (that might have been useful, might have honed me some debating skill). Instead I squandered time on an excessive focus on his faults, the needle-thin dig, the sarcastic reply, just that one beat away from impudence. Baiting him while he was sweet and distracted, generous and optimistic. In comparison to children nowadays, I did know my place, was not disobedient or problematic. But that is not a defence of my adolescent rudeness.

The Prophet Muhammad ﷺ said, 'Remember and mention the virtues of your deceased.' This comforts me because I cannot help but constantly remember my father, dream of him, see him in myself and in others. I spend considerable time dwelling on him. I am conscious of the times he lived in, the kind of education he received and did not receive, the cultural norms he operated within and at times rebelled against. The times he spoke out and the situations in which he was silent. All the things he profoundly understood, all the projects he strove for. The ways in which he was progressive and the positions in which he was traditional. His aspirations and his loyalties.

There was my father, the youngest son born and bred in Omdurman losing his mother at the age of two. Sleeping in the open air, eating with his fingers, playing football in the alley. There was my father at Trinity College, Dublin – a child runs across the road to rub his arm and then looks down at his fingers in surprise. There was my father walking barefoot through our house in Khartoum, my feet are exactly like his feet. My father stopping the car on the way back from work to buy a watermelon and bananas, being harangued by his oldest sister, at the edge of his seat because Manchester United were winning. There was my father a teenager in the 40s, a university student in the 50s, a father in the 60s. In all these black-and-white photos, he saw life in colour and things around him, through his eyes, were modern.

People often say, 'My father taught me this and my father taught me that...' Parents teach all the time, every second, every minute, but the child can only understand what echoes within her own soul. And different children pick up different aspects, translate and misinterpret, extrapolate, revise, reinterpret. Sometimes I phone my brother and ask, 'Why did Baba do this or why didn't he do that?' My brother's answer would sound like a memory of an aspect of my father that I had forgotten, an angle I overlooked. I keep remembering, gathering details, making connections, understanding better. Playing the game, 'I am now the same age as he was when this, that and the other happened...' It goes on and on because a whole life cannot be lassoed into a single explanation.

In the Botanical Gardens // *John Harvey*

Too well behaved by half, don't you think?
Policed by staff with saws and pruning knives,
they're not allowed to get above themselves.
Those that become too big for their roots
are soon cut down to size and wheeled away,
fresh little upstarts planted in their place.

And so like minor royalty, here they stand
protected from the rigours of real life.
No rain, no sweltering sun, no cutting wind
can undermine their green complacency,
and I suppose it's right it should be so,
their function after all – to be observed.

Me? I dream them clambering from their beds
like triffids, flaunting their precious flowers,
sheltering outrageous birds and beasts
in landscapes that are only partly real.
Perhaps they've reason to be arrogant
if only that they come from far away.

Scurryfunging

Rik Gammack

Scurryfunge (verb; US dialect, 1800s): to dash around the house in a frenzied attempt to tidy up before visitors arrive.
– Susie Dent, Word of the Day

Mum's call awoke Ben from blurry sleep, but what brought the world into focus was her announcement that she and Dad would be arriving in about two hours. Since it was a nice day, they'd decided to drive up, meet him at his flat, and take him to lunch. Lunch was good – he hadn't had a proper meal since leaving for uni – but letting Mum view his flat... He looked at the debris from last night's gaming session and groaned. Dad was cool, but Mum would go off the deep end and lecture him for the rest of the visit.

He fetched a roll of bin-bags and began. The low table was covered in empty beer cans and multi-faceted dice, character sheets and burger boxes. A bong stood in the middle, surrounded by a party of wizards and warriors. The game paraphernalia went back in its case, the rubbish in the bags. He hid the bong and lit some incense, then followed it up with a blast from the air freshener Mum had included in a box of essentials she'd gifted him at the start of term. He'd known it would come in useful eventually.

The kitchen recess required a bag of its own for all the empty boxes, packets and mouldy fruit. The forgotten milk, now tinged green, oozed from the bottle and splodged into the toilet; he added plenty of bleach and hoped for miracles. He piled the dirty dishes beside the sink, decided washing them would take too long, and hid them in a cupboard instead. He kept aside two mugs to wash and put away beside a third he never used, the one with the SNP logo which Mum had also considered essential.

Dirty clothes were stuffed into his rucksack; stratified layers of books and papers on his desk were straightened; DVDs were returned to their boxes. The lump under the bed-cover turned out to be a lost shirt and not a bra as he'd hoped.

Finally, he decided it would have to do. He'd get off with a heavy sigh and a shake of Mum's head. He'd been too busy to have breakfast but last night's session had included a pizza delivery and he'd saved the leftovers for later, along with a bag of cheesy puffs. It wouldn't ruin his appetite for lunch. Roast beef at the pub? His mouth flooded at the thought. So long as he got rid of the evidence before Mum arrived, a snack would be okay.

He was slumped in his armchair, reaching for his first slice of pizza, when he remembered Kate's leaflets. The boxes were in a neat, inoffensive stack; it was the contents that needed hiding. He squeezed them into the hall cupboard in reverse order, so the half-empty box from the top now sagged under the weight of the others. He pushed the collapsing stack back and forced the door closed.

He had just resumed his seat when the doorbell rang.

'Cooee!' Mum called through the keyhole. 'It's only us!' Only Mum standing on the landing shouting through his door. He had to get her in before any of the other students heard her. 'Hurry up! I need a pee!'

Panicked, he hid his breakfast in the only place available: under the cushion. He'd have to remember when he sat back down but first he had to let Mum in before she made further mortifying announcements.

Mum gave him a peck then vanished into the loo. Dad took off his coat while looking around. 'Nice. You seem to be making yourself comfortable.' He leaned forward to study the poster of a female barbarian fighting a demon. 'That isn't the one you have back home, is it?'

'Different artist,' Ben explained and, when Dad asked, pointed out the differences.

'You need more toilet paper,' Mum announced as she reappeared. 'And I left the door open to get rid of the smell of bleach; it was enough to make my eyes water. I take it you've been scurryfunging like mad since my call, but you can't do it all in five minutes.' She looked around. 'Still, not bad. I'd expected worse.' Then she glanced at the poster and harrumphed.

'Kettle's on,' Ben said before she passed judgement on the woman's bikini armour.

As he took the mugs – including the SNP one – from the cupboard, Mum said she'd brought biscuits, but fortunately added: 'Don't bother with a plate; we'll eat them out of the packet.'

Dad took his mug and three biscuits then plumped down on the armchair before Ben remembered to stop him.

Something popped and a plume of orange powder burst from between Dad's knees. 'What...?' He groped under the cushion and retrieved the bag of cheese puffs, now split open. 'Well, no point in wasting them,' he said, and began eating.

'With the size of your behind, I'm surprised there were any whole ones left,' Mum snarked.

Ben hoped Mum wasn't going to start niggling Dad about his weight; it would ruin lunch. Instead of responding, though, Dad explored further and found the pizza box.

'Something else to keep you going.' Mum wasn't letting up.

Dad opened the box and examined the topping, now adhering to the underside of the lid. 'Roadkill with extra cheese,' he determined. 'I'll wait.'

'So what else have you squirrelled away?' Mum asked as she delved between the cushions on the sofa. She found an orc, a USB drive, and Kate's missing bra. She dangled the bra from one finger.

'Ah...' Ben gargled.

Instead of giving a lecture, Mum simply sighed. 'You're a grown man now, Ben. So long as you're washing your own sheets you can do what you want. Well? What's her name?'

Ben groaned inwardly; the inquisition had started.

'At least tell me you know her name.'

'Kate.'

'Is she at uni too? What's she studying?'

'The pub sometimes runs out of beef,' Ben diverted, looking at his watch. 'I'll tell you later, but if we don't hurry we'll get caught up in the lunch crowd.'

'We wouldn't want that,' Dad said, getting to his feet and giving Ben a wink. 'Come on, dear. You can interrogate the lad over lunch. You put our coats in here, didn't you?'

A hurried 'No' escaped Ben's lips as he leapt to intervene. 'I put them –'

Dad opened the cupboard door and the tower of boxes toppled forward. One landed on his foot, Dad yelped, the box split and glossy leaflets slithered across the floor.

Mum, unsure whether to laugh or sympathise, picked one up. 'Kate Hancock,' she read, then glanced at him. 'Your Kate?'

'Yes. Look, don't worry about this, Mum.' He plucked the leaflet from her fingers. 'I'll tidy up later, after we've been to the pub.'

She bent and picked up another while giving him a sideways glance. '... for President of the University Conservative Association?' She put on her disappointed look. 'Oh, Benjamin!'

Ben nodded glumly; so much for a quiet family lunch.

If I Told You // *Judith Taylor*

If I told you, you'd go mad

so I'm not going to tell you.
As simple as that.
Life will go on just like before. But I know
I will feel lonely, here
in the house with you, in the kitchen with you
in conversations

with what I know now
between us like a membrane
or a pane of water: words pass through,
hands pass through when we touch
but we are in two
different places.
My heart

has taken one step
from the top of our building.
I can feel it falling,
feel how the air slips by
as it drops, telling itself so far so good
outside your windows, as the ground
comes up to meet it.

Gloaming // *Robert Ramsay*

Sweet fragrance on the soft night air, a
pin-prick of light, the western star and
a last straggle of cloud's mute chord,
modest, self-effacing; not a word said.
Time for worship, for memories
of those old widow-women bereft
of everything, of all they loved; none left
building and rebuilding our hospitals and schools,
communities, no authority nor tools,
their firm determination. I pause now
in this gloaming of my life to ponder,
inhale those memories in this night air
chock-full of love, and wonder how.
Their raggle-taggle old carry-bags stuffed
with knitting, crochet and tapestry,
pots of home-made jellies, trowels and secateurs,
the rocks on which our communities stood.
Oh! I feel good.

La Minotaura

Brenda Conn

Finally, we met the daughter of the minotaur. After an eternity of waiting. Not in a labyrinth, or a cave or even sitting on a rocky shore. Nothing so ordinary. No. Shopping at Tesco! Like a regular human.

I recognised her immediately, though I'd never before set eyes on her. Blood always sniffs out blood. Her glass-green eyes were mesmerising, the exact shade and shape of Aunt Ariadne's, fringed with the same luxuriant coal-black lashes, shocking against the pallor of her cheeks. My heart stopped. Aunt Ariadne, in her voluptuous youth, had been just such a beauty, same ruby lips, same fiery, Titian locks. Just like her mother, our grandmother, Pasiphae, the slut; the adulteress who went behind the King's back and fornicated with the bull. Everyone knows how that ended.

All Pasiphae's children were gifted with beauty, all except *him* – and our mother, the one no-one's ever heard of, the dispensable one. Mama never had any claims to beauty but her half-brother might have had his charms, for Aunt Ariadne went willingly to the minotaur's lair – but, of course, labyrinths always fascinated her. So eager was she for the chance, she pushed Mama aside and took her place. Triumphantly, she led the nervous band of sacrificial virgins to their fate. She didn't, of course, *share* their fate. *Her* bones never littered the minotaur's lair. Her lovely young flesh was desecrated in quite different fashion. That's always been a family secret, *btw*. Zeus knows, there's enough of Aunt Ariadne's dirty linen aired already. But here before us was the living proof.

La Minotaura would be a showstopper anywhere on the planet. Hell, she'd be right at home on Mount Olympus with our illustrious relatives – might even knock Aphrodite off her pedestal. She was dressed for the part too: her statuesque frame draped in a column of seawashed-green silk, the exact shade of those captivating eyes. Her alabaster skin needed no adornment – her perfect décolleté, long, marble-smooth limbs, inherited from mother and grandmother, beyond parallel. She looked flawless, thanks to that double dose of goddess DNA, but she was, without doubt, her father's daughter. That purest of pure white skin for a start. Then, there was the tail. Undisguised, it swished flirtatiously with every long-legged step, the tip a flag of flaming scarlet. And the hooves, gold-varnished, glittering, they drummed down the supermarket aisles. Fab-u-lous!

But Tesco? How could the grandchild of a goddess stoop to that? Nothing remotely ambrosial on the Tesco shelves. OK, Theo and I were shopping there and we're Pasiphae's grandchildren too but, like I said, our Mama was the anony-mous one, no god-like powers for us, just an eternity of scraping by. Same old, same old, as they say these days. Homer would have put it so much better but Theo and I have to move with the times – and we have to eat. Largely vegan for us in these modern, environmentally aware times. We slip by, anonymously, unnoticed in the crowd.

Not like La Minotaura. Heads turned in every aisle as she stomped towards the butchery counter. Unopposed, she barged to the head of the queue.

'Ten kilos of your finest, *freshest* sirloin.'

Our cousin's deep, sonorous voice reverberated throughout the store, carrying all the horrors of the labyrinth, paralysing shoppers and staff. The counter assistant's face turned a greenish shade of pale.

Her father's appetite and manners, we noted. All thought of introductions vanished. Then, she inclined her head towards us and *sniffed*.

At the Top of Night // *Todd McEwen*

In older days thou drunkard
they'd command your spirit removed
from your pink and empty fag-smoked vessel
gaping alone on the upper deck of the night service
to dance alongside as best it could:
your little soul trying to keep up
made to race trip and stumble
through the terrible world of the night roofs:
breaking slates, hopping jagged guttering
up and down the corbie steps to wave to you.
It dodges sleeping animals
smashes face first into chimney pots
calls out, falls, gets skewered
on thistle-shaped Scottish spikes
at the peaks of black haunted dormers.
Only later could it skulk into the house
and crawl back into your body
as you slept on the shore
of a drooled, lapping lake.

Medusa // *Kim Crowder*

I'm the slippery streamered scourge of the sea / mad-maned / gelatinous gorgon / long-lost cousin of the corals / bag-body / beach-bogey / venomous star pulsating / nerve-netted / elastic lobed / placental jelly umbrella / boneless bell / brainless gob / going with the flow / tangle with me and you'll lament the lash of my tentacular touch / pre-dating dinosaurs / dining on small-fry / predatory plague of the paddlers / I'm heartless.

A Puckle Mindins

Rachel Matheson

Mindin Een: Strammely, shitey wee pieces o reid twine. Rippit an knotted, plunkit awa in a tin wi a daft picter o a castle glowerin an fauchie-lookin on the lid. Wee tin, something fur shortbread or ither nonsense, the noble landscape it eence depictit hazed ower an miserable wi rust. Sat on the fireplace.

The village wis sma an there wis een street, wee sidey lanes peelin aff it intae stumpy ends like a hunk o seaweed. A time weel afore the grandbairn, barely afore the dother. Peggy's hauns are coorse, even then, bit nae rigid, can cut through the air like a scurry doon the herber, shuckin guts fast as yi'd blink.

The manny she's mairriet tae moves mair canny, tumbles ben the village at the pace o a hivvy kert missin a wheel. He belongs on the watter, can slither through updraft o spumin waves like a siller fluke if needs be, bit, on land, aye glances aboot fae beneath his bunnet like some daft crab movin wi scuttlin agitation ower the shore, anxiously keekin oot fae unner its shell at aw times. Aye apart fin on land, her man. Even their waddin day he's lookin oot at something tae the side in the anely photie they hiv, speerin at some circlin danger, a reason fur caution.

'Oh, the fisherman's a bonny bonny man
Ah've ne'er seen onything bolder...'

He is bold at sea, bit, regardless, ilka time he leaves, Peggy maks him sit by the kitchie table wi his airm oot an ties her wee length o reid skein roon his wrist. Sharp, gratin stuff it is, fierce eneuch tae withstaun the waves. She sings as she winds an ties.

'An they ca me the fisherman's lassie...'

Dark een aat swallow up the gaze fae her siller, he peers doon at the twistit leathery folds o his ain palm, wrist circlet wi dark hair tanglin amon the reid. His cigarette smoke aets up the pale licht comin in aff the sea an smothers the room. Fin she's done wrappin her charm tichtly roon him, he stands up, stiff as a trunk, an walks tae the door, pausin tae nod at the wee manny Jesus, limp on the crucifix, een fisherman tae the ither. Een wye or ither, some auld religion will keep him staunin oot there, some charm encircle him agin danger.

A fierce end tae April aat year, a hackin hoast o sudden sna pouder, clairtin the coastline an aetin up the shore. Fur three day aifter the storm subsided, she gid doon the herber in the bitter caul, sun mak'n a diamond glint oot o the cruel lift. She watched an she wited. She wore her ain reid band, a threid sewn intae her thick socks fur luck. At

Rachel Matheson • 29

the kitchie table she sat, speerin oot o'er the kickin waves, scowlin ower at Jesus intermittently through the fug o her Woodbine finiver she caucht him eein her up fae the crucifix. She wited. Then, fin eneuch time hid passed, she hung the mirrors backward.

The bairn came wi'in five month. Twa year aifter aat, she readied hersel tae flit, tae boot her sorrow tae the granite buildins faarer sooth. The wee dother, Marie, born wi the epilepsy, fit the doctor cried the 'Sacred Disease', bletherin aifter some auld Greek nonsense, a cursed result o the faither's daith maist likely, some said. In the Toon, they micht mak her better, shift the lingerin sickness o his ghast, cure tham baith o the grief.

Fae the cottage, she'd te'en Jesus. Aneath him, the nicotine an the scowlin kitchie smoke o their short lives thegither hid left an imprint, a cross markit on the plaister like a snaw-ghast, a phantom o the blizzard ye couldna trust. An she'd te'en the wee tinny fae the fireplace in which, ilky-time he returned safe, he hid cut the charm she'd gien him an deposited it.

Ilky bliddy time.

Bastard.

Getting Personal // *Brenda Conn*

I am not a people person I have been told
by someone who is and so should know.
I am a people person she said
and *you* are not.

I ponder this and wonder
what kind of person am I
if not a people person?
I like people. I am a person.
I am person who likes people.
But I am not a people person?

The person who told me I am not a people person
was adamant. She is a people person. I am not.

I stood on her doorstep, clutching
flowers taken by way of apology
for possibly having caused some offence.
She did not want my flowers.
She did not want my apology.
She had no interest in dealing with a person
who was clearly not a people person
other than to set that person straight
on her non-people-person status.

That done, she took the flowers and shut the door.

Beware // *Leela Gautam*

Hypnotised, mesmerised, propelled by lies,
we implode to nothing as democracy dies.

Land of the free, strong and great,
weakened by peddlers of greed and hate.

What matters our wealth, faith and learning,
when reason is shaken, and freedom lies burning?

False, those prophets who conspire and plot,
to change the landscape our fathers wrought.

Beware! Beware! We could lose it all,
it is from within that nations fall.

A Na'vi for the White House

Roger Meachem

Breaking News: USA PRESIDENTIAL CANDIDATE
STELLA MARCH, FOUNDER OF TRUTH NOT
SCIENCE, HAS BEEN ABDUCTED

'Serina, where did it all begin?' Something sensational was in the wind; Arlene felt it in her bones. Serina Pittendreich, director of one of the world's most successful franchises, had never before given an interview.

The slight woman dressed simply in a white skirt and beige jacket replied quietly and confidently. 'It began in my garage, of course, Arlene. Don't all mega-corporations begin in a garage?' She paused, then, 'I'd phoned the police to have them deal with Andrew....'

'Your husband.'

'The crook stealing from our charity, *Clothes for NHS Staff*. I got pushed from one extension to another and had about given up hope when I got to speak to a real person,

"Sorry, Mrs, Pittendreich, since the efficiency cuts, we're pretty much overwhelmed." I remember how the officer dropped his voice. "If it's not an attempt to overthrow the Government, you'd best go private." So, I did.'

LORD GAST OF GAST FOUND FROZEN TO DEATH
The Chairman of one of the UK's more notorious energy companies is discovered inside an industrial sub-zero refrigerator dressed only in running shorts and trainers.

'You attempted to have your husband murdered.' Arlene's broad Scots accent rolled the 'r's.

'I didn't know any better and hired a cheap hit-man. The fool met with Andrew in a pub, put poison in a pint but got the glasses mixed up.'

'So, you took matters into your own hands.'

'Indeed.' Serina paused as though reliving the experience and smiled. 'I dealt with Andrew in the garage. That was when it occurred to me. Here I was, twenty-seven-years old. Better at the assassination lark than the cowboy I'd hired. I spent the night putting together a business plan while rendering Andrew down. In the morning, I was in touch with the bank. I called my company *T Cell. Bespoke Assassinations.*'

'Yes, umm, T-Cell...?'

'T-Cells! They seek out harmful antigens in your body and destroy them.'

Arlene grimaced. Thousands could be switching off at

the mention of two scientific terms in one sentence. 'Your company, T-Cell, began the wave of assassinations of those considered a danger to *The Body* – the population of the UK. Who made the decisions as to the targets? You?'

'Not at all. Social media helped me reach out to those with that information. I used a simple metaphor. "Humanity is a body. Criminals are destroying that body, destroying our future. T-Cell can destroy the destroyers. You can help us by contacting SOS@TCell.com. Think of your children. All information is treated with the utmost confidentiality." Cases came flooding in. Even the UK business was too much, so I began the franchise.'

WeSLINGIT OWNER DOUGIE PERTWEE FOUND DEAD FROM STARVATION, TRAPPED INSIDE LOCKED ROOM
The fast-food company is notorious for its low wages

SEARCH FOR STELLA MARCH NOW NATIONWIDE
There has been no ransom demand. Hopes are fading.

'You weren't the first Private Assassination Company, but you've proven to be the most successful. Where do you go from here?'

'Well, Arlene, that's why I'm giving this interview. Assassinations are expensive, and those who know about deserving cases can't always afford to get it done. I realised that social media provided me with both information on who needed retiring and finance – crowdfunding. It helped that I gave extra incentive.'

'By providing assassinations where the target got an end that reflected their crime?'

'Absolutely! Do you remember the trebuchet case?'

'Moby Mac? The multi-millionaire loanshark?'

'Boss of Icarus Credit. He boasted there were no heights to which he wouldn't descend to reach his goals. We shot him from a trebuchet built under his roof-top sun lounger. We'd intended Moby to reach the Serpentine, but the wind had dropped, and the prick bounced off the Albert Memorial. Screaming to the last, I'm told. So, back to my decision to allow this interview. T-Cell has always kept ahead of its competitors, and today I'm announcing our next project.'

Arlene noticed her technical team leaning in, anxious not to miss a word.

Serina wafted a floating speck of dust away from her skirt. 'We're moving part of our business into drone technology. Most tasks can now be carried out remotely and very, very cheaply. T-Cell's well-trained human teams will re-dedicate their skills to simple enforcement. You see, Arlene, there are large numbers of people who, though they attack the Body of Humanity, probably don't deserve to be boiled in custard, dropped into the in-chute at a cornflakes factory or stranded on a mountain during a thunderstorm while wearing metallic long-johns. No, thanks to our drones, we'll continue with our standard range of terminations, but now we're beginning to tackle errant souls before they err too far.'

'Examples?'

'Just read today's news headlines. We've already begun.'

LORD TOOTING KIDNAPPED

A week after suggesting that the UK bomb North Korea, Tooting's private yacht appears to have mistakenly sailed into North Korean waters with Tooting aboard. It is not known if the hawkish UK Defence minister is still happy.

USA PRESIDENTIAL CANDIDATE RESCUED

Following a nationwide search, Stella March has been found, after being kidnapped by a Jake Sully cult. Covered in blue dye and wearing only a thong, Stella says she no longer seeks the Presidency but wishes to return to her home planet with the Na'vi. Crowds of similarly dyed and unattired supporters have appeared outside the hospital where she is being treated, carrying posters demanding 'A Na'vi for the White House'.

China Rose: An Exclusive Design by Roy Kirkham
// *Haworth Hodgkinson*

Whenever I went to visit
I was welcomed with Earl Grey or Darjeeling,
but never until China Rose had been found
from wherever it hid when I was away.

This beaker – nobody in Lancashire would use the word mug
to describe an item of fine bone china –
would remain in use for the duration of my stay
and return to storage when I went home.

My mother collected Roy Kirkham designs.
She had sets of English Rose, Redouté Rose,
but only this one China Rose,
its ornate red and blue flowers outlined in gold.

I'm not sure how it came to be associated with me
but I was happy to play along with the ritual,
and on my final visit, when she was no longer able,
I had to search for it myself in the front-room cupboard.

A year on from my mother's passing,
China Rose has found its way to my Aberdeenshire desk
and as I work, sipping Assam orange pekoe,
I have to admit a certain fondness for the beaker I'm using.

A Growing Friendship

Martin Walsh

(chapter from a novella)

Señor Bacalao was a private man; he was always courteous
to his customers but he kept himself to himself. The only
soul who had grown remotely close to him in Zaragoza was
Señora Cigüeña, his most regular customer. She was the
Dueña of the café bar diagonally across the street – appro-
priately named Café de las Cigüeñas – which had recently
gained a reputation for the quality of its seafood tapas. It had
taken the Señora a long time and great tact to break down
Bacalao's reserve; but, once she had succeeded, he rewarded
her with his friendship and helped her business flourish.
Indeed, it was he who sourced her seafood, making a rare
exception to his normal fixation with cod. Occasionally, and
only if there was no wind or sunshine in the street, Bacalao
would cross Don Jaime Street. There he would drink a *café
cortado* and munch *churros* at the bar counter behind which
the Señora served.

She had been a customer of Bacalao's for almost two
years before their friendship blossomed. A casual remark,
made one morning in his shop, changed the nature of their

acquaintance for ever. She startled him with the observation that she had seen him in the Rio Ebro the previous afternoon, during siesta time. He looked at her for some moments before speaking. 'But it was raining hard and there was no-one by the river; I checked.'

'Maybe so, but did you look up?'

He looked at her, mystified. 'In the trees?' He couldn't somehow imagine her climbing a tree.

'No, not in the trees,' she laughed, 'and where did you learn to swim like that? I thought you had drowned! You were under so long I was worried. And when you came up, you were 100 metres up-stream!'

For the first time since the Señora had met him, he looked troubled.

'Don't worry,' she said, 'your secret is safe with me!' She picked up her dried cod and glided elegantly towards the door. 'And remember,' she tapped the side of her long nose, then broke into the serenest of smiles, 'now you know *my* secret too, so we are in each other's hands!'

Bacalao had turned her words over and over in his head but they made no sense. It troubled him that she had seen him swimming, that she might share his secret with others. But nothing happened. She continued to visit regularly, their conversations remaining business-like and friendly. On one occasion she said: 'You should come across for a coffee one morning, when you aren't too busy.'

'You are kind, Señora, but I must decline!'

'Suit yourself, Señor Bacalao, but I would so love to lift that frown from your brows!'

'I don't know what you mean.'

'You will know soon enough.'

Bacalao remained confined to his shop until the next rains
came. There was hardly a soul on the street. He donned his
long black raincoat, pulled up its collar, covered his bald pate
with an everyday beret and locked up his shop, turning the
sign on the door from *abierto* to *cerrado*. His Seat 500 was
in a lock-up two blocks away. It was the kind of car no-one
noticed: cheap, common and easy to forget. However,
for such a large being, it looked incongruously small. An
observant bystander might have found something comical
in the sight: Bacalao cramming his bulky, slope-shouldered
body into its interior, that little barbel quivering on the end
of his chin just above the steering wheel. But there wasn't a
person to be seen.

Bacalao's domed forehead almost touched the wind-
screen as he peered through the flaying wipers at the road
ahead. How he hated this new-fangled one-way system.
His destination was only just across the river, a little further
downstream from where he lived; yet to reach it he had to
drive miles in the wrong direction. Even once he had crossed
the Puente de Santiago to the north bank, he had to loop
away from the river before rejoining it at his chosen quiet
spot on the outskirts of the city. He parked the Seat under a
willow in the Parque de Oriente. There were no other cars
in the park and nobody to be seen. He locked the vehicle
and strode towards the river, following the Paseo de la Ribera
until he reached a wooded corner by the confluence of the
Ebro and the Río Gállego. A sign by the river read: *Corrientes*

peligrosas, no bañarse aquí – dangerous currents, do not bathe here.

After checking that no-one was around, either on the river bank or in the trees, he quickly stripped off his clothes and hid them under a bush. That's when Señora Cigüeña's words returned to him: 'But did you look up?' He gazed up into the rain-smudged sky. A few birds: some swallows swooped over the water for insects and above them a small flock of circling storks. He shook his head; what the hell was he expecting? The tall figure of the Señora somehow levitating over the river? Or might she be on a broomstick? Ridiculous! Breathing in deeply, he plunged into the Ebro, barely rippling its surface. In his element at last, he felt the cool water racing along his flanks, smelled its smells, savoured its tastes. It felt like home, almost... But he had to be careful – the gel with which he covered his body only protected him for so long. He made straight for the turbulent waters where the two rivers joined, corkscrewing through them with the easy grace of a dolphin. When finally he emerged, precisely at his starting point, he glanced around him.

Nothing had changed. The rain was still falling, the banks remained empty of people, the swallows continued to hawk for insects, the storks were still milling overhead. Absently, he noticed that one of them had detached itself from the group and was flying low, its beak inclined towards him. *Was it watching him?* The bird clacked its long bill like a castanet then wheeled off to join the other storks. *Strange,* thought Bacalao, as he hauled on his clothes; then promptly put it to the back of his mind.

The next morning, once the café's breakfast rush had passed, Señora Cigueña crossed Calle Don Jaime to visit Bacalao. After the usual pleasantries she looked him straight in the eyes, her long nose pointing squarely at his barbel: '*Estimado Señor*, never in all my years have I seen a man swim with such power and grace.'

Once again Bacalao looked stunned, his equilibrium unravelling. In the ensuing silence he searched his memory for clues, playing back yesterday's swim in the Ebro, and her enigmatic remarks over the past weeks. He looked at her anew. His eyes narrowed, then flashed suddenly with a strange green-gold fire and an expression of dawning yet perplexed recognition: 'That stork? That was you?' The frown on Bacalao's brow lifted, to be replaced by something rarely seen.

'How good to see you smile, Señor. So now will you come to my café?'

Bacalao gazed at his neighbour with something akin to awe. 'It will be my great pleasure. I will come when next my business is slow and the weather is right.'

'I shall await your coming with impatience.' She moved to the door in long elegant strides, like one of those tall, emaciated models on a catwalk, turning in the doorway to utter a friendly '*hasta pronto.*' That was the beginning of their friendship, a friendship between one who could swim like a fish and another who could fly like a bird.

In Passing // *Mary Cane*

I know what it's like to hold two opposing ideas.

When I pass a grown-up son in the car,
one part of me is happy
that he has a home, a job, is married.

But the other part checks the rear-view mirror,
in case he is reversing regardless of traffic.

In case he wants to reach out and touch my arm,
look at me with his father's eyes and say:

'Hi Mum'.

The Sigh // *Mary Cane*

At the bottom of my lane there lives a sigh.
	I know because I hear it every time I pass by.

Odds

Zusana Storrier

His name's not Roy, but it'll do for now. We bumped into him again last night, as we came out the Co-op.

Pre-plague, Roy would stalk the reduced-to-clear section. Now his son has food delivered to him and none but Roy has gone into his flat for nine months, but he still stands outside the shop, looking at the brightly lit aisles and tugging at the edges of his mask.

'You don't need to wear a mask outside,' I said by way of greeting, as we stepped off the pavement to leave more space. He followed us into the gutter. Like many people who've played in rock bands, his hearing's eroded to the visual, even at night.

'Can't be too careful,' he said a foot from my face, the fabric sighing over his mouth.

We both had covid, Iain and I, back in the spring. It wasn't much of an event for us. Roy, however, is just the age, and size, to take it badly. The Pretender to a Ventilator Iain calls him. There was the mask at least, luffing in and out, but it's only been a week since I was in the city, in two double-deckers and a stuffy room. For all I know, despite the previous exposure and the precautions I've taken, I could be hoaching. We moved further into the road. And Roy came too.

'Off home?' he asked.

'Bargain-haul. Got a Yule log for 45p.'

Before I glared at Iain, I glimpsed pain pass through Roy's eyes.

I said goodbye, maybe hastily, and realised that Roy wasn't leaving.

'Where the hell do you live now?' Roy said as we all returned to the Square.

'Same place as always.'

'Why aren't you going there?'

I looked at the vast lichens of ice covering the pavements down the brae. 'I thought you wanted a walk.'

'Why would I want that?'

'Don't know, early New Year resolution or something.'

With the exception of the circular route around the Square, our town is all hills and valleys. To get to our house from the centre you have to go down the steepest brae then back up the other side of it. At this time of year, both slopes are white with trodden ice. Roy was wearing his slippers. These are the type that look like moccasins but are made from maroon fabric and have a foam sole. Roy told us once that they saved a lot of bother when he went to the shop.

'You'd better watch if we go down the brae,' I said, aware of sounding like a care-worker, which is what Roy used to be.

He ignored me.

Iain coughed and Roy and I looked at him, for different

reasons. 'We *could* go down Park Brae instead,' Iain said. Park Brae takes you to the burn at a kinder angle, but with a longer journey, and has a factory that grits the road for its vehicles.

Roy wandered on and off the pavement as we descended. When he spoke, he swung into the crunchy road, when we replied he jostled us to make out what we were repeating in the street light. My shoulder scraped along the factory wall, Iain fell behind. I saw Roy's gut lurch off orbit as his feet slid over patches of frost.

The three of us gaped at the path beside the burn. By now Roy's mask was covering his nose only and was inside-out, the white lining showing. 'Oh, fuck it,' he said, peeling the strings from his ears and throwing the contraption like a collapsed bird onto the polished floor of black ice, 'I hate these bloody things.'

'There's no way you can get along that in your... shoes Roy. I'm sorry, but we need to go back.'

'Bugger that,' he said, and pushed off as a treble-sized Reverend Walker on Duddingston Loch.

Fat men may seem protected from falls and knocks by their reckless flesh, but elbows, knees and crowns still sport bone just below the skin. I imagined the clunk of Roy's head off the ice-glazed asphalt.

We, Iain and I, struggled to keep up and keep upright. Roy pitched forwards, backwards, to either side, but stayed on his straddled feet, or a foot, sometimes a yard ahead, sometimes five. Whenever I tried to catch up, he speeded his reeling. I was itchy with sweat by the time we arrived at the foot of another path, one going uphill.

This path is the sheerest in our steep town. Past trees, over the tops of trees, it needles straight to meet the big-brae road. Last night it was a 150-yard-long ice-slide. Roy slithered to the handrail, let go and began huffing up the stiff grass on its far side, seemingly very pleased with the strategy.

'Oh Jesus,' whispered Iain, 'he's a heart attack in slippers.'

'Take your time there, Roy,' I shouted. I let distance sag between us in the hope it would slow him.

When he reached the first group of trees, he took hold of a bole for a few seconds. He doubled over as he pushed off.

'Roy,' Iain bawled, 'there's no need to rush man.'

'Used to do... plenty of... wiping arses... must do... more...'

We were running now, up the frozen grass, out-of-breath ourselves.

'...Ro-oy...'

As he cleared the second grove his head disappeared and his shins and slippers were in the air. I think I put my gloved hands to my mouth. I know I dropped the Yule log. When I'd blinked, he was thrashing like a tipped cow. But then he was on his feet again, agile – somehow – around that belly.

'...No... no...' He held up a quivering palm as he clicked his knee straight with the other hand.

'Are you alright?'

'Eh?... Oh yes... perfectly.'

There were ten yards of ascent left. Roy began a bellow which became a roar and held his elbows up like a five-year old at sports day. We were both awestruck to see him reach the roadside railing and clamber over it, belly incised by the top rail, thunderous noise still spilling from his throat.

When we got to the pavement, however, he was mute, gulping air. What would we do if he was fibrillating? We couldn't offer him a supporting arm, not these days. CPR, the kiss of life – what a thought – all out of the question.

There was the sound of an engine coming up the brae. Could we stop the vehicle? No, probably we couldn't. We'd have to phone.

But now he straightened like a man half his years. 'Feel fine.' And he stepped nimbly onto the road.

Both over-illuminated decks of the bus flooded my sight. Iain came from behind, grasping for Roy as our companion turned his head over his theatrically lit shoulder and saw the Number 20.

'Bloody hell,' Roy said. Yet he seemed to saunter away as the vehicle grazed the side of his jacket with a tearing noise. Iain tumbled onto the frozen tarmac the bus had vacated.

In the bus-less darkness Roy tried to examine his jacket pocket. 'I might have to sew that.'

I'll say this, Iain was on his feet in seconds.

'Do you want a cup of coffee Roy, in the garden like? That was quite a shock.'

Roy sniffed, all breathlessness gone, 'Nah. Too risky sharing crockery. At my age I've a ten percent chance of dying of covid. Thanks though. Think I'll just head home.'

Hope // *Sarah Jane Toleman*

During the gale
the rowan tree fell,
branches splintered
roots exhumed,
turf torn.

Yet the roots clung to the soil,
dug in deep,
took long draughts
of ditch water.

The branches stretched
grey mossy limbs
across the grass,
secretly swelling buds.

Spring in the shattered forest
was scarce
but the black tips
unfurled miniature fans
amongst the undergrowth.

With Gratitude // *Sandra Davison*

I am before you
who stand tall, though
on reflection perhaps
slightly crooked – life-worn
but still and strong,
sturdy and enduring.

Reaching towards you,
my fingers touch your limbs
and trace your wrinkles,
sensing your tenacious resolve
to survive – come what may.

The rain stirs around us,
a gentle blurring – or is it
my tears?

I look up at you,
my heart filling with gratitude
as I see the glen around us,
reflected in the delicate
tears balanced on your needles.

The Philosophers

Andy Fairnie

Trying to sleep through the cacophony of pre-dawn night wasn't worth the effort. I learned that the hard way, and quickly. My cell mate, the cunning Benjamin, had learned that too, long before me.

So, every night of survival, we sat on the dusty floor, cross-legged, spinning verbal webs around ourselves; impervious webs of philosophical protection, a home-handy-man version of Kabbalah. Our amateur philosophy was not professional, not spun like the thick webs over our bunks; webs that hung between the lines of cotton thread that Benjamin had rigged a couple of feet above the sheets as a cunning framework for spiders to weave and spin, creating the perfect mosquito trap. Thanks to Benjamin's ingenuity and the innocuous reel of cotton thread he had, somehow, carried into captivity, we were spared the buzz and bite of mosquito hell that kept younger guys awake at night. Trapped in their cells, grappling with fears for their own mortality, and driven crazy in seemingly everlasting circles of purgatory, those poor lads howled and begged, night after night, in a choir of misery that echoed across the jail from sundown till the first precursor of dawn. That choir fell inexorably silent at the very first gunshot of the grey dawn's executions.

Then we slept, another night survived.

Stranger Danger // *Ian Anderson*

Haud aff fae strangers, they said at skweel
a bobby cam and telt us jist the same
but I didna need nae tellin.

In yon days my auntie bocht me comics
gart me pick them at the paper shop
an ae time there I met a loon.

A wee laddie fae her close
nae muckle aulder than masel
but cam the day he nivver made it hame.

I doot he went wi a stranger,
my auntie telt my mither
whisperin an tryin nae tae greet.

It wis sax lang weeks efter
they cam on him at last
beeried like a beast anaeth a fleer.

He micht hae been ma freen as we grew up
but he hid gaun wi a stranger.

The Parcel

Martha Craig

The boy rings the bell and waits on the doorstep; and waits ... and waits ... This is no good. They're waiting for him now to join the five-a-side. He'd rather be with his pals. He's looking forward to today's game. They'd played against the Bay Boys before. The teams were evenly matched. Today's match would be the decider. Becoming impatient, he starts to tap a foot. What can he do now? Can't even return the parcel.

The well-dressed stranger had approached him just down the street from here and asked him to deliver it. Before he could refuse, the parcel had been thrust into his arms, a twenty-pound note into his hand and the stranger had turned and walked swiftly away. Twenty pounds! The astonished boy had thought, 'Oh, well. It'll only take a minute. I'll still get to the game on time.'

He gives a sigh and catches his lower lip in his teeth. Though he has no watch, he's aware of the minutes ticking by. He moves from the doorstep to the ground-floor window, but it's too high for him to see inside. There's a small garden bench further along the wall and, putting the parcel on the doorstep, he drags the bench to the window, climbs on and stands up. He sees what seems to be an empty room. Shading his eyes with one hand, he can now make out some cases near the far door. Beside them stands a woman with her back to him. Some instinct causes her to turn round and when she sees the lad, she leaves the room. He hears the front door being opened, then her booming voice. It comes so suddenly that the boy almost loses his balance.

'What are you doing out there? You gave me the fright of my life!'

He points to the parcel.

'I was supposed to give you that.'

As she snatches it up and slams the door, he jumps from the bench and starts to run; but he still hears her screams as they echo from the empty house.

The Horses of Fair Hills // *Peter Noble*

The horses of fair hills
stand steady, seeming to know
more than we can guess, at rest
in fields where telegraph poles
stretch onwards and upwards.

The horses of fair hills
gallop for the joy of being free;
hooves pound the hillocky fields
into favourable ground,
inviting them to gather.

The horses of fair hills,
heads bobbing up and down,
look to the future
as they wait for owners
with projects and plans.

The horses of fair hills
would hope that the fields
will always be theirs and
the hills will never grow old.

We Were Rich // *Martha Craig*

We were rich when we were children,
rich in time, to daydream and to make-believe.

Town-bred, yet rich in freedom of fields,
woods and sea: free to crash silently down
sand dunes, run the sun-speckled shore,
scream with gannets and gulls.

Rich in the lore of living and dying:
the cat-killed bird, cold and head-slack, buried
with reverence; the farmyard piglet, overlain by sow,
final resting place a manure pile.

In bluebell woods, an ancient oak: its canopy
home to scampering squirrels, busy-winged birdlife;
saplings born of seed from dying branches
nourished in its soil, sheltered in its shade.

The Key

Charlotte Thomson

'I'm not sure about this, we might get caught.'

Jake turned the key in the lock. 'Don't be silly, Catherine, there's no-one about.' He stumbled into the hallway. 'Too late now, I'm in!'

Hesitantly, she followed, the yale lock clicking behind her. The smiling faces of a handsome couple, young, middle-aged and older, beamed from a line of photographs in the hallway. The living room was exactly as Catherine remembered it; four bright-yellow chrome-framed chairs sitting neatly round a coffee table. A geometric-patterned rug accentuated the length of the room, leading her eyes towards a brown Swiss Cheese Plant drooping below an impressive oil painting. She recognised the woman from the photographs in the hall but here she was posed, un-smiling, formally attired in a shimmering black gown. Why so serious? Catherine's musings were interrupted by a sudden bang. Jake was at the cocktail cabinet, the opened door still juddering.

'Interesting,' he said, motioning her over. 'Not sure what this is but it still smells decent.'

'Jake – we had enough at the pub. We were only coming in for a peek. I really think we should be heading home.'

'Where's your sense of fun, Cathy? One drink – just one *teensy-weensy* drink?'

She caved, sat down, glass in hand, found the yellow chair surprisingly comfortable. 'Bottoms up!'

The sweet amber liquid slipped down and before long Cathy's eyelids felt heavy. She sank into her chair watching the last rays of the summer sun dance along the wood-clad walls, scarcely stirring when Jake suddenly bounded from the room.

Whistling, he clambered upstairs, floorboards creaking at every step. A few minutes later he was back, eyes sparkling. 'I noticed this last time.' A large cardboard box landed with a thud, spilling sequinned fabric.

'You need to try this on Cathy. You love this vintage stuff.'

'Amazing! It's the dress from the painting!' Wriggling out of her blouse and jeans, she tugged the dress over her head, sequins and tassels fluttering.

'Have a look at the rest, sweetie, while I fix us a top-up.'

Colourful frocks, bracelets, long strings of pearls, dainty shoes, travel souvenirs and an old stamp collection tumbled to the floor.

'Cheers,' Jake handed down her drink as she knelt on the carpet, rummaging through the box. 'When I saw them packing those dresses last time, I knew you'd love them.' Jake pulled out two fluffy pillows from the bottom of the box. 'Remember the fun we used to have, before the kids?' He tossed her a pillow. 'Duel!'

Fuelled by amber nectar, the challenge proved irresistible. Catherine stumbled to her feet and entered the fray. Jake was too quick for her as she chased him round the room, ducking out of shot but landing his own attacks with accuracy. In minutes the air was alive with feathers. She collapsed on the floor in a fit of giggles.

'So... pretty... jus' like a shnowshtorm... Gemme 'nuvver lil drinky-winky, love...' She hiccoughed. 'Oops!' Hiccoughed again. 'We gotta get this sorted... go home...'

Catherine drifted into consciousness, blinded by pain, blinking in the dazzling sunshine. Her back ached and she felt weighted to the floor; *where was she?* Realisation dawned.

On the ground lay their scattered clothes; the dresses and bric-a-brac from the box; a carpeting of feathers. She poked her snoring husband, a grumble the only response. She poked harder, jumped to her feet, dressed quickly and began frantically making amends. Jake was pulling on his jeans, still only half-awake when they heard the doorbell.

'Wha...at?'

'Hell's bells...'

'And precisely who are you?' A woman with a shrewd little face appeared in the room, barging past a still-sockless Jake. 'This doesn't look right at all to me. You're not relatives of Muriel's, are you?' She waggled an accusing finger, her curls bouncing in indignation. 'I'm warning you – I'm calling the police this minute unless you have a *very* good explanation. Muriel was my neighbour for fifty years and I've never set eyes on you two before.'

'Sorry… you're right. I know this looks bad… but we're the new owners… we were just celebrating…' Catherine's voice tailed to a whisper.

'The new owners? Nonsense. Why, it hasn't been sold yet.'

'Well, not officially, but our offer was verbally accepted yesterday, and we'll be moving in soon.'

'A likely tale! And how on earth did you get in? It's only the estate agent and myself with keys.'

Jake looked sheepish. 'The agent gave us the keys when we viewed the house last week. They were pretty loose on the keyring and… well, one must have fallen off into my pocket before I handed them back…'

'Enough. Do you think I'm a fool? I'm phoning the police.'

'No, *please!*' Tearfully, Catherine explained it had been a moment of madness on a night of celebration, assuring the woman that normally they would never behave so out-rageously. Their toddler daughter, little boy and baby-sitting parents, Jake's difficult upbringing and all-round lack of ill intent were proffered for no police involvement.

'And it would be such a shame for poor Muriel's family if this place is on the market any longer than need be,' Jake added. 'Calling the police might complicate things… with getting our mortgage approved….'

Seeing the woman begin to soften, Catherine butted in, 'The estate agent told us they're desperate for a quick sale, with all the care-home bills.'

'Yes, well, that's true enough, and it would be a shame for us to get off on the wrong foot. I'll turn a blind eye – so long as you leave right now.' The stern frown evaporated, replaced by a surprised smile, as Catherine lunged forward to hug her neighbour-to-be, before hustling Jake towards the door.

'Not so fast... I'm Mary Brown... *Miss* Mary Brown, from two doors down, number 23... and you are?'

'I'm Catherine and this is my husband, Jake Mulholland – thank you for being so understanding, Miss Brown. We'll be off now.'

'Wait,' Miss Mary Brown was not quite finished with them. She stretched out an imperious hand towards Jake. 'Don't forget the key.'

Pauses at an Arisaig Window // *Bernard Briggs*

Morning clouds stretch above
a row of white, grey-slated buildings.
Loch nan Caell a mirror: toy yachts.
A sail bangs a mast. Below our house
a crow mobs a white chicken.

Late afternoon, the light is flat:
watercolours on taut grey muslin.
A dinghy is being rowed slowly
from the shore, avoiding a skerry.
Hard is black, soft is silver.

Sunset dresses above Rhum and Eigg.
The yachts are still there; the rooftops
the skerry, the dinghy now moored.
The mirror has gone and the moon arcs
in faded, denim blue and pink silk.

Letterbox Caves

Gayle Burgoyne

We don't know why we've come here, we don't know how we'll leave. When our paths converged, we reached for each other without a care for the crosswinds. Now we can't let go. Don't sit there by the stile, you haven't the time in your life. The mind can't comprehend all this shattered rock.

Have you seen the wrens who make their homes in the letterbox caves? Do they know it's only pelts of moss and roots of pioneer birch holding the quarry tips together? Too quick for the eye, wrens will survive the collapse, don't you think?

I like to notice the yellow. Gorse isn't obviously inviting but if you risk a prickle you'll be rewarded. Coconut, can you imagine? I like to glimpse the time before. Reminds me to hope for an after. Time to move on now. The ravens don't wait for carrion, we're told. They call foxes to open the bodies of those who have surrendered.

Catkins, look. Male and female still perfectly in tune. A shame about the bees. Can the wind pollinate? I used to know so many things about the world. That was a different world. The ground is no longer the ground, they say, just an intermediate layer in how we have been stratified.

All this slate formed south of the equator. The last bare peaks rise out of a plate that drifted north from tropical zones... If it's a kind of return we're experiencing, I think I'm all right with that. I wish it weren't so fast.

Lichens are the first to colonise inhospitable lands; their decay after death formed our early soils. Stuck on the outside of spaceships, in legions they died in tests. We never did find out whether they'd survive on Mars.

Barbed // *Knotbrook Taylor*

The day after you died, men in blue hats with long narrow spades came and put up a fence.

They arrived in the afternoon, as though to give me the morning for my reflection, and worked on into the evening.

The next day at dawn I saw the finished device. Bright, taut-stretched, jagged; humming with the breeze.

Blocking me from the birch and pointed pine; from the flight-lines of crow and kite.

Blocking the us and the we. Trimming the sky from the earth. Singing with the wind a new, and unasked for, song.

Feral Funeral // *Kim Crowder*

Dog-fox, trotting, pausing on black-stockinged tip-toe, scenting,
fox-trotting, following: blood-bonded to the track. Gunshot!
Echoing one shot. Scapula smashed. Pelt, blood-matted, persists
shamefully splayed, run over and ruthlessly over: degraded.

Prise the parched scab of him: release, retrieve, take every trace
for overdue rites. Amongst wild funereal flowers, in fern fronds,
shroud him. Let fumitory – smoke of the earth – shade him.
With wood-sorrel assuage. Mourn him – and all the woods' feral
deities defiled.

A Murmuration // *Marisia Kucharski*

A murmur at the fraying edge of day,
a winged sigh sweeps across the half-lit sky,
in monochrome crescendo, it lifts;
space expands, contracts
or perhaps we rise towards
to close the gap   grown so vast
so fast   diminuendo carries
us gently back
through crest and trough
till bereft, clinging
to the dying
wave and the hope
our desire won't fade,
we inhale the silence,
this colossal gift, this dance
around time, our chance to hold
the rush of the roar, embed it deep,
sense the axis tilted,
feel the thrust of the raw,
the unrehearsed exposed;
let it be   a lesson please
and maybe we will pause,
consider our position,
nudge ourselves
off centre stage, open up
our narrow field of vision,
hear in a murmur how we might soar.

Biographies

Leila Aboulela
Leila Aboulela's most recent novel, her sixth, is *River Spirit*. Leila was one of the original Lemon Tree Writers in the 1990s. Her *Tuesday Lunch* was the first story work-shopped.

Ian Anderson
Ian writes poetry in Doric and English, and is greatly supported in his scribbling by his wife and fellow Lemon Tree Writer Dominique, their dog Harvey, and their five cats.

Bernard Briggs
Sussex born, has produced four collections of poetry. His work has also appeared in numerous anthologies and magazines, both online and in print.

Gayle Burgoyne
Gayle writes novels, short stories and essays exploring the strangeness of human reality, and runs creative writing workshops to help connect with the world beyond the human. More at: gayleburgoyne.com

Mary Cane
Mary invents through writing, painting and curating. She works with everyday materials, words and memories. These coalesce in different ways. Sometimes as here, in poetic form.

Brenda Conn
LTW member since 2014. Writing highlights of 2023: Wheedling

with 'proper poets'; a Granite Noir author badge as a 'Local in the Limelight'; a poem published in Poetry Scotland.

Martha Craig
Martha's work was first printed in her school magazine. Since then, many of her pieces have appeared in minor publications. Her first book is now available on Amazon.

Kim Crowder
Kim lives and writes in Angus between Strathmore and the Grampians. She is a descendant of Thames Watermen, washerwomen, chars, chancers, and cockneys, plus Kentish, Irish and Scottish farm labourers.

Sandra Davison
Sandra has been a LTW member for several years. A recent creative writing newbie, she plans to explore through words and photographs what tàmh (Scottish Gaelic for dwelling, quieting) means.

Andy Fairnie
Andy is a father of seven, a globe-trotter, and a creative wordsmith. Fuelled by patriotism, he savours life's pleasures: food, wine, and the great outdoors. Let the adventures continue!

Rik Gammack
Rik is surrounded by notebooks and pencils. If the muses ever whisper in his ear, he'll be ready. Until then, the books contain doodles of airships and reminders for wine.

Leela Gautam
Leela's poems have appeared in PoetrySpace.co.uk, in Tim Saunders publications and in Aberdeen Inner Wheel journals. She was invited to read a poem at the 2022 Edinburgh Festival.

Eddie Gibbon
Economic migrant from Liverpool during the Thatcher purges. Five poetry collections published. Accepted and rejected by many magazines. Allegedly Byronic (Stuart Kelly in *The Scotsman*). Inaugural chair, Lemon Tree Writers.

John Harvey
Though he was born in Edinburgh John has lived in Ottery St Mary (Devon), Chelsea, Brummana (Lebanon), Dewsbury (Yorkshire), Arran, Reswallie (Near Forfar), Dundee and now lives in Meigle.

Haworth Hodgkinson
Has produced two collections of poetry and 28 albums of music, largely concerned with the changing seasons, landscape and people of the North of Scotland. More at: www.haworthhodgkinson.co.uk

Marisia Kucharski
Marisia hopes her writing acknowledges both the failure of words and their conjuring magic; that despite falling short, words can reach outwards, ask who are you, are you human too?

Todd McEwen
Todd McEwen was born in California, educated in New York and somehow washed up in Scotland in 1981. His latest book is *Cary Grant's Suit*. He lives in Edinburgh.

Rachel Matheson
Rachel is a disaster. She'd blame Portlethen, if she could. Her story, *A Puckle Mindins: Mindin Een*, is part of a longer story awarded the Toulmin Prize 2023.

Roger Meachem
Roger's default-personality settings as a writer are humorous, mis-

chievous and quirky. Serendipity is his favourite noun and you'll find him where the wild things are.

Peter Noble
Peter is a golfing poet who enjoys poetry with a sense of place. He is grateful to Lemon Tree Writers for many years of shared stories.

Robert Ramsay
Glasgow University, civil engineer West Africa, dredging. Farming in Angus, Governor Rossie School. Retired. Gardening, poetry, published four books, 20 years Lemon Tree writer, Speakers Club member.

Zusana Storrier
Zusana's short stories often centre on unobtrusively disadvantaged and obliquely rebellious characters and have been published in British and North American anthologies and magazines. She lives in Kirriemuir, Angus.

Judith Taylor
Lives in Aberdeen, where she co-organises the monthly Poetry at Books and Beans events. Her new collection, *Across Your Careful Garden*, is out now from Red Squirrel Press.

Knotbrook Taylor
Angus poet. Winner 2014 Erbacce Prize for *Ping-Pong In The Rain*. Other books include *Scottish Lighthouse Poems (*2011), *Beatitudes* (2007), and *The Year Of The Lark* (2022). More at: www.knotbrook.co.uk

Charlotte Thomson
Lives with her two cats and ever-patient husband. Works in journalism but loves to escape the real world by spending time in nature plotting storylines for her naughty characters.

Sarah Jane Toleman
Sarah Jane has been writing poetry for ever, though only recently dared to share her awe and delight in the natural world and hopes to inspire the same in others.

Martin Walsh
Marine biologist, Kentish Aberdonian, writer of short stories, long-term devotee of LTW. Favourite themes: Magical Realism, Africa, Latin America, wildlife, memoir, absurdity.

'The End of Poetry' by Eddie Gibbons was first published in *What They Say About You*, Leamington Books, Edinburgh, 2010.

An earlier version of 'A Mention of my Father' by Leila Aboulela was published in *Jalada Magazine*.

'Getting Personal' by Brenda Conn was previously published in *Poetry Scotland*, Spring 2023

'Odds' by Zusana Storrier first appeared in the Elphinstone Institute Lockdown Lore archive.

Thank-you to all our wonderful members, past and present, those featured in this anthology, as well as those who are not – every one of our members contributes to making Lemon Tree Writers the supportive and vibrant writing group that it has remained since its inception 30 years ago.